Albert Bradburn Barrows

**Jim Bullseye in Boston**

A Dialect Poem

Albert Bradburn Barrows

**Jim Bullseye in Boston**
*A Dialect Poem*

ISBN/EAN: 9783337409036

Printed in Europe, USA, Canada, Australia, Japan

Cover: Foto ©Andreas Hilbeck / pixelio.de

More available books at **www.hansebooks.com**

# JIM BULLSEYE

### IN

## BOSTON

## A DIALECT POEM

### BY

## ALBERT BRADBURN BARROWS

ILLUSTRATED BY

### EDWIN FORSYTHE PORTER

RESPECTFULLY DEDICATED

TO THE

Massachusetts Department

G. A. R.

# INTRODUCTION.

JIM BULLSEYE, fresh from his ranch by the Rockies, visits Boston for two purposes : first, to take part in the Grand Army Encampment proceedings, hoping to see familiar faces of comrades who, during the War of the Rebellion, shared with him the vicissitudes of life in camp and field ; and second, to thoroughly inspect the old town of Boston, of whose culture, energy, wealth and Puritan principles he had heard so much.

Arriving in Boston a week before the opening of the Encampment, ample opportunity was afforded him to thoroughly explore the city.

On the evening of August 13th (the night following the grand parade) our hero stands just inside the door of Mechanics' Building (Camp Phil. Sheridan), his pants tucked into his high-topped boots, his broad-brimmed slouch hat pushed slightly toward the back of his head, a pipe in his left hand, his empty right sleeve pinned up.

He is peering intently and curiously into the faces of those who pass in and out. Suddenly he steps forward and accosts a new-comer — a well-built, nicely dressed man, of decided military bearing, some ten years, perhaps, younger than himself — in the language embodied in the first lines of the poem.

"Don't you know *me* — Jim Bullseye — Pard?
You hain't forgotten *Jim?*"

Page 7.

# JIM BULLSEYE IN BOSTON.

Hullo thar! Say! It 'pears to me
  I knew a chap like you
Away down South in Dixie's Land,
  In sixty-one an' two!
Don't you know *me* — Jim Bullseye — Pard?
  You hain't forgotten *Jim!*
Ole Time ain't worked no frightful change
  In neither you nor him!

O' course we ain't so young an' pert
  As when we used to swipe
Ole Hans von Doozen's sausages,
  An' Larry Hogan's pipe!
Your eyes don't look so sharp — your ha'r
  Is gray — an' as for *me,*
I somehow sorter don't seem quite
  So young as I used to be!

## JIM BULLSEYE IN BOSTON.

Do you remember the fun we had
  With the sooperstitious nig?
How we nigh about got mustered out
  For stealin' the sutler's pig?
You hain't forgot the fearful night
  We took that twelve-mile tramp,
When our fingers froze, an' our tattered clo'es
  Hung heavy with mud an' damp?

How Corp'ral Tom took sick, an' 'lowed
  He'd never see the sun?
How you carried his knapsack all the way,
  An' I his belt an' gun?
We didn't dream how bad he was —
  But he petered out that night,
An' we closed his eyes for 'im — you an' me —
  Jest as 't was growin' light!

Do you remember the army mule
  What we called Ob-sti-nate?
W'ich his eyes wor so awful little,
  An' his ears so awful great?

D'ye recollec' the voice he had?
　His vocal apparatus
Was out o' plumb — so said the boys —
　From singin' "Inflammatus!"

Now, what that was, or what 't was like,
　I never 'zactly knew;
But he sounded like he was inflamed,
　So I allus s'posed 't was true.

They say one time he stretched his face
　Near a churchyard, jest at dawn,
An' the dead folks riz an' 'gun to dance,
　A thinkin' 't was Gabr'els horn.
But when they saw ole Ob-sti-nate,
　They felt so kinder cheap
That they pulled the bed-clo'es over 'em,
　An' went straight back to sleep!

＊　　＊　　＊　　＊

## II.

I thought as how I might, per'aps,
　See some one what I knew

If I took this 'ere Encampment in —
    An' I 'm mighty glad t' see you!

Now, set right down on that thar stool,
    An' fill this ole T. D.,
An' smoke in mem'ry of the time
    When last you smoked with me!

\*    \*    \*    \*

### III.

An' so you 're livin' here, you say,
    Married an' settled down,
With little folks what call you dad,
    An' make you stan' aroun'!
What! Visit *you!* I 'd like to — but
    I could n't act polite : —
I 'm nothin' but a backwoodsman,
    With an awful appetite!

I 'm full o' dust — my ha'r 's uncombed —
    My boots ain't greased or shined!

I 've no more manners nor a b'ar,
    Nor any more refined!

You really *want* me for to come!
    An' your wife — she 'd like me to!
An' I would n't scar' the chil'ren!
    Wall, I 'll tell you what I 'll do:
I 'll visit *you* tomorrow, if
    You 'll visit *me* tonight!
So straighten back, an' cross your legs!
    That 's biz'ness — here 's a light!

      \*    \*    \*    \*

### IV.

Wall, after we wor mustered out —
    Some time in sixty-three —
I hardly reached the North afore
    I went straight back — d 'ye see!
You did the same! That 's jest like you!
    An' did n't lose a limb?
But why do they call you Kurnul Bob —
    An' me plain Privet Jim?

Whar's my right arm?  That's in the swamp!
  I left it whar I fit!
Two Johnny Rebs are layin' thar,
  A sorter guardin' it.
I don't min' tellin' how 't was done,
  Although the yarn's a short one:
'T was in a little picket fight —
  But 't was a mighty hot one!

The night was awful dark, an' I
  Was on the outer line,
When all to once a sense o' dread
  Came flittin' through my min'!
An' list'nin' thar, I plainly heard
  The soun' of an army's tramp;
So I fired my gun at random like,
  To rouse the sleepin' camp.

The Johnnies knew its meanin', an'
  They made a frightful din,
As they rushed in all the'r fury, for
  To drive the pickets in!

"An' list'nin' thar, I plainly heard
The soun' of an army's tramp."

You never heard, in all your life,
  A more blood-curdlin' soun'!
It was as ef the clouds had bust,
  An' ev'ry foot o' groun'
Had opened up, an' all the imps
  Of air, an' sea, an' hell,
Had stretched the'r mouths, an' let out one
  Tremendous, frightful yell!

I tried to load my rifle, but
  Afore the job was done,
One Rebel's sword was raised at me,
  An' another Rebel's gun.
'T was death or prison for Bullseye Jim!
  I sized it up — d'ye see!
So I clubbed my gun an' went for one,
  While t'other came for me!

Wall, never min' what happened then!
  'T is not a pleasin' tale,
An' ev'ry time I think of it
  I kinder sorter quail;

For though it was in battle done,
　An' all in self-defence,
I 've had the feelin' like I was
　A murd'rer ever sence ;

An' when the fight was over, an'
　The ambulance came roun',
I only thought o' them two Rebs,
　Aside me on the groun'.
An' when I saw 'em layin' thar —
　So still, so white, so dead —
With all my soul I wished to God
　It had been *me* instead!

An' I made the fellers promise me —
　Thar by the ole turnpike —
That they 'd git the chapl'in to say a pra'r,
　An' bury 'em Christian like.
So the boys they up an' humped 'emselves,
　An' brought out Parson Joe ;
An' he prayed a pra'r, as he stood thar,
　That reached God's ears, I know.

He telled the Lord all 'bout this 'arth,
   An' all the sorrer in it,
Way down from Adam an' Eve'ses time
   To that same blessed minite.
He dwelt mos' mighty hard, they said,
   On the war then goin' on;
If *some* had heard 'im, they 'd a wished
   They never had b'en born!

For if God had n't known afore
   Jest whar the blame should lay,
He knew it *then*, for Parson Joe
   He gave it dead away!
Then they hollered a grave both deep an' wide —
   So said the boys what seen 'em —
An' they lowered 'em into it, side by side,
   With my right arm atween 'em.

An' when ole Gabr'el toots his horn
   To wake us all — d' ye see!
I can't help hopin' them thar Rebs
   Will give my arm to me.

V.

Wall, yes, I saw the big parade,
　　An' marched myself, to boot!
It *did* seem kinder strange at fust
　　To hear the bugles toot!
But when the bands begun to play
　　The good ole war tunes — then
I somehow kinder seemed to feel
　　I was a boy again!

But what a crowd turned out that day!
　　How well the boys all marched!
Although some on 'em made me think
　　Of ole shirts, newly starched!
They stood it well for a little while,
　　But they had n't strength to last;
An' one by one they dropped from line —
　　The'r marchin' days wor past.

But I mus' tell you 'bout one man
　　What looked mos' awful bold:
His boosom gleamed with badges, Pard,
　　Of silver, bronze an' gold!

"I somehow kinder seemed to feel
I was a boy again."

Page 16.

An' I said to a feller standin' near:
"What gen'ral's that?" said I;
"Whar did he git his glory frum?
    Whar did he bleed an' die?"

An' then the feller grinned, an' said:
"D'ye mean that ancient plum?
He stayed in the rear with a fancy band,
    An' fit with the big bass drum!"

Wall, jest behind him limped a chap
    On crutches — one leg gone!
He looked as ef he might be tired,
    An' his face was kinder drawn;
But thar was somethin' 'bout his looks
    W'ich sorter *jest took me*,
An' p'intin' to the one-legged man,
    I asked who he might be!

"Oh! That's Ben Jones! No flash 'bout *him!*
    D'ye see that tattered rag?
Wall, when they charged Fort Donelson,
    'Twas *him* what carried that flag!

He fit for all his soul was worth,
   An' lost his leg right thar;
But all the badge you 'll see on him
   Is the badge o' the G. A. R.!"

Wall, when I looked at th' struttin' cock,
   An' roun' at the other — then
I turned my back on the spangled cuss,
   An' gave three cheers for Ben!
Now, aint it kinder sing'lar how
   Real worth hides out o' sight?
An' how the dog with the biggest bark
   Has allus the smallest bite?

\*    \*    \*    \*

## VI.

How do I like your ole Bay State?
   Wall, now, in point o' size,
'Longside o' some I 've travelled in,
   She don't seem much — leastwise,

If my ole sheep an' cattle ranch
  Could jest be sorter raised,
An' dropped on this ere Commonwealth —
  I guess you 'd be amazed!

Why, Gosh-all-hemlocks! Sure 's you 're born,
  I 'd bet my ole slouch hat,
Thar would n't be 'nuff margin left
  To more nor braid a mat!
But she 's a State to be proud of, though!
  She ain't all talk an' bustle!
She puts her han' on her *pocket-book,*
  An' then things have to hustle!

An' when the bugs eat up our crops,
  An' blight destroys our grain,
An' cyclones come — we look to her —
  An' we never look in vain!
God bless the ole Bay State, say I!
  Blood tells, an' allus did!
An' chil'ren o' the sires *she* raised
  Won't leave the'r candles hid!

### VII.

But *Boston!* She jest s'prises me!
  Why, I 'd no sorter notion
That your ole Pilgrim 'tropolis —
  Here by the 'lantic Ocean —

Was sech a right smart bit o' place!
  She 's really quite a town!
'Pears like I 've seen more people here,
  A prowlin' up an' down,
An' more good-natur'd fun a goin',
  Likewise more money spent,
Than I ever saw at a hangin'
  In a Western settlement!

I hain't seen much o' poverty,
  I hain't seen much o' crime,
The little w'ile I 've b'en here — p'r'aps
  It ain't so all the time.
Thar ain't no place but what, I s'pose,
  Has plague-spots here an' thar,
An' Boston prob'ly has 'em, but,
  I don't know whar they are

"Your fakirs an' your hucksters,
   Sellin' ev'ry 'arthly thing."

Page 21.

The winders o' your shops an' stores
  Look wond'rously invitin' —
Especially your pictur' shops,
  For pictur's I delight in;
An' when I strike some funny thing,
  Why, then I laff right out;
An' it 'mooses me to hear folks say:
  "What 's that fool laffin' 'bout?"

An' then some solem'cholly thing
  Heaves to, an' 'fore I know it,
My face grows long as a broncho's head —
  An' that 's the way I go it!

Your blin' ole fiddler — playin' tunes
  On one dyspeptic string,
Your fakirs an' your hucksters,
  Sellin' ev'ry 'arthly thing —
An' mostly sellin' them what buy;
  The'r tongues forever wag
With "Gollar buttons, five a piece!"
  An' "Peanuts, five a bag!"

But worse than all these janglin' soun's
    Is the blamed, infernal din
What 's made by aggravatin' boys
    With bent-up bits o' tin!

\*    \*    \*    \*

### VIII.

Your colleges an' institoots
    All fill me with amaze;
They 're far beyon' my humble speech,
    An' far beyon' my praise!
Your Mooseum o' Fine Arts, an'
    Your Nat'ral Hist'ry Rooms
Jest take a feller all the way
    From ole Egyptian tombs —

With mummies tied in 'tater bags,
    An' pree-hysteric bones,
An' gran' ole pictur's, cracked with age,
    An' glaz'er whitened stones,

Down to our nineteenth cent'ry time,
　With all its wealth an' power,
Jest like as ef this good ole 'arth
　Was on its weddin' tower.

*     *     *     *

### IX.

Your Public Garden makes me think
　Of Eden in all its glory,
'Fore Adam an' Eve wor ordered out ; —
　You 'member the Sarpent story?
Your houses all are beautiful,
　Your public buildin's grand,
An' Parson Brooks'es Meetin' House
　Beats any in the land!

But Trin'ty allus makes me think
　O' one o' the human race,
Whose back was han'somer by far
　Than ever was his face :
In front she 's grand, an' on the sides
　She 's sweet, an' still she 's bold ;
But in the rear she 'minds me of
　A poem writ in gold!

I never saw a buildin' what
  To me seemed quite so neat;
An' I bought a camp-stool t' other day,
  An' squat thar in the street,
An' watched the birds in the ivy leaves,
  An' many a cooin' dove
Fly back an' forth an' in an' out
  O' the peek-a-boos above.

But the teams they bothered an' pestered me
  As I sot an' admired it thar;
The p'licemen howled, an' newsboys yelled:
  "Git onto the grizzly b'ar!"

\*     \*     \*     \*

## X.

You 've got some bang-up places here
  For folks with appetites;
An' somethin', too, to wet one's flue,
  An' help wash down the bites.

"Bring me," said I, "some *mee*-noo!"
An', I added, "Have it rare!"

Page 25.

Thar 's the Vendome Tarvern, f'r instance —
  Jest a splendid place to browse —
An' Mr. Brunswick's feedin' s'loon,
  An' Thorndike's boardin' house.
I' ve tried 'em all, an' rather like
  Their pushtiveness an' vim ;
But they 're jest a little steep in price,
  Leastwise for Uncle Jim.

The fust time what I sampled one,
  I was hungry as a b'ar;
An' I looked the program over
  As I dropped into a cha'r.
Wall, the food was French an' Latin,
  An' I thought to get my fill
I had better take a send-off
  With the fust thing on the bill.

So I called the colored waiter,
  An' assoomed a knowin' air:
" Bring me," said I, "some *mee*-noo! "
  An', I added, " Have it rare! "

Then the waiter snicker-giggled,
  An' he mumbled somethin' 'bout
How they 'd had a rush on *mee*-noo,
  An' *mee*-noo was all out!

He asked me if I would n't like
  A plate o' *de-foy-grass,*
An' a slice o' *corn-so-may,* well done —
  Said I: "Young man, I pass!
A Yankee dinner is what I want!
  Your foreign grub won't do!
Jest bring me somethin' I 'll understan',
  An' bring it P. D. Q.!"

Then he humped himself, an' trotted out
  Some eyesters, fish an' roast,
With puddin' an' pie an' cake an' sech,
  An' hummin'-birds on toast!

'T was too nice thar for a hoss like me,
  With only jest one fin,
An' I could see the dashin' swells
  An' han'some ladies grin

At the awkward work I had to make,
  As into the food I sailed;
But when I riz thar was nothin' left
  *Exceptin' what was nailed!*


\* \* \* \*

### XI.

Your graveyards fill me with a sense
  Of what New England was
When them whose names are written thar
  Wor framin' of her laws.
To show respect for sacred dust
  Is all that one can do;
An' I allus doff my ole slouch hat
  When a graveyard heaves in view.

Coz them ole Pilgrim fellers what
  Are mould'rin' an' sproutin' thar,
Had jest the sand what saved our land,
  An' made us what we are!

'T is true the'r views wor narrer, but
   I think that may 'ave come
From walkin' in the narrer streets —
   It must a helped 'em some.

\*    \*    \*    \*

### XII.

Now, speakin' o' streets, I 'm awful 'fraid
   I can't say much in praise;
You hardly orter call 'em *streets* —
   Mos' of 'em 's only *ways!*
O' course, you have a few nice roads,
   W'ich some call av-e-nues,
With purty trees, an' walks so broad
   That folks *can* walk by twos.

But them 's the 'ception; one would think,
   In biz'ness parts the town,
The streets wor cut from remnants, an'
   They would n't half go roun'!

An' when a man with shoulders broad,
   An' feet in like propo'tions,
Attempts to turn an' face about,
   It calls for skilful motions
To keep from smashin' winder-glass,
   An' runnin' chil'ren down ;
So I have to wiggle sidewise when
   I 'm walkin' through the town !

But worse than bein' narrer, is
   The'r crookedness — d' ye know,
They 'd take the crookedest kind o' prize,
   In the crookedest kind o' show !
One feller spun this yarn — said he :
   " The cows o' Chawmouth town,
In goin' to an' from the'r barns,
   An' prancin' up an' down —

" Fust made the pathways, now called streets."
   But that song would n't do !
He could n't stuff your Uncle Jim —
   I 've seen a cow or two !

Thar never was a fool-cow yet,
  In common sense so lax,
W'ich same would go to Mexico
  To get to Halifax!

Wall, I hit upon the cutest plan
  O' gettin' through the town:
I went an' bought a compass for
  To fin' my way aroun'!
My compass looks some like a watch—
  It only ain't so grand!
An' somethin' like your Uncle Jim —
  It's only got one hand!

An' when I turn myself about,
  Some sorter 'traction rocks it;
So, I've b'en an' hired a sailor for
  To learn me how to box it;
An' 't won't be long afore I'll know
  The whichness of the how;
It's easy: Nor'-nor'-west by east,
  Or west-nor'-east by sou'!

So when I want to fin' a place,
  An' my head begins to whirl,
I ask a boy, if one 's in sight —
  If not, I ask a girl!
('Coz men an' women gab so much,
  An' take so long to do it,
That oftentimes I walk away
  Afore they half get through it!

But boys an' girls, when asked a thing,
  Don't talk all roun' about;
They tell me if they know — if not,
  They say so, out an' out!)
An' when they p'int me, then I take
  My compass from its nest,
An' box it — sou'-sou'-west by nor',
  Or nor'-sou'-east by west!

    \*    \*    \*    \*

### XIII.

I thought as how, bein' here, d' ye see,
  I 'd better "do" the town;

An' I kalkerlate, as fur's I know,
   I 've done the job up brown.
I 've " taken in" your shops an' mills,
   Your factories an' stalls,
Your churches an' your galleries,
   Your stoodios an' halls.


I went all through your biggest stores,
   An' I could swar — d' ye know,
That the popilation all turned out
   A shoppin' for to go!
But one thing what I noticed was,
   Nine-tenths the people went
To ask for things they did n't want,
   An' would n't spend a cent!


But what jest took my breath away,
   An' gave to me the gripes,
Was the double back-action, patent roomatic,
   Stan'-without-hitchin' pipes!

" Was the double back-action, patent roomatic,
Stan'-without-hitchin' pipes!"

Page 32.

What, take your money, an' bring the change,
  Without no talk or clack,
Without no cussin' — nothin' but
  A slap-bang — *gone!* An' whiz-pop — *back!*

An' I could n't help lookin' frontwards,
  To the time what p'r'aps is comin',
When they 'll use roomatics for to send
  Us human folks a hummin'!

An' what with gas an' 'lectric lights,
  An' steam an' 'lectric cars,
An' dynamite, an' glycerine,
  An' beans! Why, bless my stars!
This 'arth will have to hump herself,
  Or she 'll git so mighty slow
That we 'll have to board some other craft
  What *can* git up an' go!

\*     \*     \*     \*

### XIII.

I was strollin'. roun' about the wharves,
　　Quite early, t' other day,
An' I j'ined a 'scursion goin' out,
　　An' started to " do " the bay.
The air was mild, the sky was blue,
　　With nary cloud in sight;
The sea was like a lookin'-glass,
　　All streaked with dark an' light.

Some o' the crowd wor playin' cards,
　　An' some wor shakin' dice;
Some hankered after trouble, an'
　　Wan't actin' over nice!

" What toughs are them ? " I asked the mate;
　　" Hush! Hush! " said he to me:
" They 're Boston Common Scoundrel men
　　A junkettin'," said he.
I looked 'em over, head to foot —
　　A hard lot, 'pon my word!
" If that 's the *common* stock," said I,
　　" I think I 'll take *preferred!*

## XIV.

I had one disapp'intment, Pard:
　I 've hankered all my days
To hear an op'ra — one o' them
　Thar grand ole singin' plays!
But the theatres wor shet; an' when
　I asked the reason why,
Folks said the actors took a rest
　When Mercoory was high.

I felt most awful sorry, 'coz,
　I 'd allus heard it said
That Boston's 'moosement places wor
　A length or two ahead
Of anything this side the pond —
　That is, I mean to say,
For doin' real, good, wholesome work,
　In moosic an' in play.

But the freak-shops all wor goin', an'
　I 'd jest as lives you 'd know
I had some fun, the other night,
　In a cheap va-*ri'*-ty show!

The fust thing took my 'tention was
   A sing'lar lookin' man,
A settin' jest behin' the door,
   An' leanin' on his han'.

He had a queer complexion — why
   His face was white an' yaller,
All 'cept his nose, w'ich same was red,
   An' shined like painted taller.
I saw as how he watched me with
   A sorter vacant star',
An' never turned his head away,
   An' never moved a ha'r.

I thought as how I'd be perlite,
   So as I was goin' by,
I nodded to him, friendly like,
   An' "How-dy-doo?" said I;
" Nice weather for the crops, ole man!
   Corn's lookin' up — so's grain! —
All 'ceptin' wheat — that's hangin' back,
   I s'pect for want o' rain!"

"So I hollered in his lef' ear, an'
I shouted in his right."

Page 37.

Wall, not one word the feller said,
  But kep' right on a leerin';
Then I grew mad, but thought as how
  He might be hard o' hearin'.
So I hollered in his left ear, an'
  I shouted in his right,
An' then got roun' furninst his mouth,
  An' yelled with all my might!

It wan't no use — he never moved,
  Nor speaked a single spoke,
But seemed to leer more leerfully,
  As ef he smelled a joke.
I raised my fist an' lent him one,
  When — Holy Cat! D' ye know,
I foun' I 'd hit a man o' *wax*,
  What b'longed to that thar show!

I then went whar folks acted in
  Some milk-an'-water plays;
Whar aged people sung an' pranced
  In very kitt'nish ways.

'T would take a week to tell you all
  Them actors said an' did;
An' I wept as I heard the stale ole jokes
  I laffed at when a kid.

I think I might a stood it, p'r'aps,
  An' waited till 't was through,
Ef it had n't b'en for an ancient dame
  What fluttered into view.
She was dressed as only a school-gal should,
  An' sung with a horrible lithp,
An' said she was dear little Buttercup, she,
  An' thweet little will-o'-the-withp!

Wall, then, I up an' asked her if
  She would n't like to send
Some message to her gran'son who
  Was livin' at Jinks'es Bend.
An' what d 'ye think she went an' did?
  You never saw sech pranks!
She jest made faces straight at me,
  Instead o' sayin' thanks!

An' then the augience laffed right out,
  The manager he swore,
An' I was invited to view the place
  From jest outside the door!

    \*    \*    \*    \*

### XV.

I 've allus wanted for to see
  A real, 'live man-o'-war ;
So I went aboard a cruiser, an'
  Some wondrous things I saw.
I had n't b'en thar long afore
  I met a Midshipmite,
W'ich told me many things about
  How them thar ships could fight.

He said as how they had one gun,
  They called the Mizzen Spar,
W'ich same at forty miles would drive
  A nail, or split a ha'r.

He said when comin' roun' from York,
  'Bout ten leagues off the coast,
They spied a Jarsey 'Skeeter, w'ich
  Was settin' on a post.

Then they loaded up the Bowsprit, an'
  The Main-top-gallant yard,
With canisters o' grapes an' sech —
  An' would you b'leve it, Pard,
He jest declared, with honor bright,
  An' 'thout no sign o' boastin',
That the fust shot killed the Jarsey bird,
  An' the second *driv the post in!*

He p'inted out the Holy Stone,
  An' said the pious tars
Jest loved to pull it roun' the deck
  An' mumble out the'r pra'rs.
They 'd had, he said, a whiskey boom,
  But the bo'sun up an' drank 'er,
An' when the vessel acted bad
  They had to jibe an' spank 'er.

He asked me if I would n't like
　　To help him splice a brace ;
An' took a flask out, quiet like,
　　An' held it to my face.
I really had a likin' for
　　The sprightly little jay,
An' I asked him for to visit me
　　If he ever sailed my way.


\*　　\*　　\*　　\*


### XVI.

But what amazed me most of all
　　Was what I saw an' heard
In the Paralyzer printin' shop —
　　Shall I tell you what occurred ?
Wall, a hop-an'-go-fetch-it lookin' boy,
　　With reddish ha'r an' face,
Consented to go along with me,
　　An' show me through the place.

We fust went up — wall, I should think,
 'Bout forty flights o' sta'rs,
Where we came across a lot o' men
 A smokin' cheap cigars.
Aroun' each feller's neck thar hung
 A great, big pair o' shears,
An' pens an' pencils, pipes an' sech,
 Wor roostin' on the'r ears.

They all looked wild an' holler-eyed,
 An' all seemed scar'd an' vext,
Jest like as ef they thought as how
 Each hour would be the'r next!
They wor in a ramblin' sort o' room,
 An' in the middle on it
Was a grin'stone — what the feller said
 They groun' the'r *pens* upon it!

An' guns an' pistols lined the walls —
 A gattlin' in the corner;
Wall, I slipped my han' roun' on my hip —
 I did, upon my honor!

"Why, this is our Editorial Room!

They 're harmless chaps," he said.    Page 42.

" What 'sylum's this ? " I whispered like ;
　The boy grew still more red :
" Why, this is our Editorial Room !
　They 're harmless chaps," he said.

I then remembered what I 'd heard —
　The tale must 'ave b'en true —
That Editors, like Congressmen,
　Would smoke whatever grew !
An' when cigars were made too rank
　To give away or sell,
Why, they were sent to Editors
　For puffs — an' hence the smell !

We then went up another flight,
　To what the Sun-burst said
Was called the Imposition Room —
　Whar lots an' lots o' lead
Was layin' roun' permiscus like,
　In little bits o' pieces,
An' men were sortin' of 'em out
　Accordin' to the'r creases !

The men were solem'choly chaps,
  An' looked jest fit to drop;
" Who are these wretches gathered here? "
  Said I to Sorrel Top:
" Them 's Average Impostors, sir;
  They 're stickin' type! " he said;
" If 't wan't for them thar would n't be
  No books or papers read!

" The reason why they look so sad,
  So tired an' full o' care,
Is on account of others' sins,
  W'ich they are made to bear.
But why they 're called Impostors, sir,
  Is past all findin' out,
Unless it 's coz they' re 'posed upon
  An' said bad things about!

" If 'dition 's late, or forms are bust,
  Or anything goes wrong,
Why, they 're the fellers what get cussed —
  It 's b'en so all along! "

"It was a wild an' mournful place." Page 45.

They wor havin' a sort o' round-up thar,
   An' things wor in a mess;
He said the 'dition was summut late,
   An' forms wor goin' to press.

It was a wild an' mournful place,
   An' brought back to my mind
That rule o' Hoyle's: " Who enters here
   Must leave his *hops* behind!"
For eve'y one, from devil up,
   Looked dry, an' like as though
He was awful anxious to see a man —
   Down on the street below!

Wall, then the boy he said as how
   He guessed we'd travel down
To whar the press put in it's work,
   In the regions under groun'.
He asked me into a little room,
   Not more than six-foot squar',
An' then he shut the slidin' door,
   An' p'inted to a cha'r.

But I had hardly squatted, when
  He pulled a little string,
An' 'fore I 'd time to pray or sw'ar,
  Down went the whole blamed thing!
I grabbed the boy, the boy grabbed me,
  An' I began to yell;
But down we went, without a stop,
  Until we came to — well —

The strangest place! It made me think
  Of an undergrounded mill;
An' thar was the great, big Jumbo press,
  A roarin' fit to kill!
The way that thing jest humped itself
  An' groun' the papers out,
Was somethin' truly wonderful,
  An' made my eyes stick out!

An' I asked the aged vill'in
  W'ich was bossin' o' the work,
How many papers it could print,
  Pervidin' it did n't shirk.

An' he said as how, when feelin' well,
　　An' goin' with all its power,
'T would print 'em at the lightnin' rate
　　Of *a hundred sheets an hour!*

　　　＊　　＊　　＊　　＊

### XVII.

'T was mighty hot the other night —
　　Not a zeffer moved the trees ;
An' I wandered out to your garden spot,
　　A hopin' to catch a breeze.

An' I gazed at the statoos, one by one,
　　An' listened to the crickets' cheep.
I then sot down on an' ole settee,
　　An' soon fell soun' asleep !

An' I drempt the gosh-all-firedest dream,
　　As I slept in that thar place !
Why, I drempt that the statoos all came down
　　An' j'ined in a friendly race !

'T was fust agreed that Washin'ton —
  Bein' the only mounted chap —
In order to use the others fair,
  Must give 'em a handicap!

I saw by ole Ed Ev'rett's looks
  That he was boun' to show
The other statoos gathered there
  Some things they did n't know.

He rolled his pants up, 'termined like,
  Kicked off his big brogans,
Pulled off his socks, turned up his sleeves,
  An' then — *spit on his han's!*

But Charlie Sumner seemed to think
  The race no consekence;
An' he took his coat off, careless like,
  An' hung it on the fence.

Then Tommy Cass unhitched his sword,
  An' went an' washed his face,
An' blacked his boots, an' brushed his clo'es,
  An' 'lowed he'd j'ine the race!

"George Washin'ton he shook hi'self,
An' climbed down from his mule." Page 49.

An' even the Ether Sick Man riz,
  With a sleepy sort o' grin,
An' said he was feelin' better,
  An' they might count *him* in.

George Washin'ton he shook hi'self,
  An' climbed down from his mule,
An' led him roun' an' roun' a spell,
  To let the saddle cool!

The Maid-o'-the-Mist she combed her ha'r,
  An' entered with the rest,—
But the judges ruled her out to once,
  Because she was n't drest!

Then suddenly I stopped my ears,
  Such a cry as heav'nward went
When the Goddess slid from her perch, high up
  On the Soldiers' Moniment!

The dew was on her garments,
  An' the dew was on her ha'r,
An' she looked too sweet for anything,
  A smilin' an' bowin' thar!

Wall, then they drew for places, an'
    Ed Everett smiled a smole
As he rolled his breeches higher up,
    An' calmly took the pole!

But Charlie Sumner, all to once,
    Began to hop an' dance,
An' wave his han's, an' kick hi'self,
    An' try to tear his pants!

It seems a tribe o' yaller wasps —
    Not little ones — but *rousers* —
Had b'en an' gone an' built a nest
    In the boosom of his trousers!

I pitied Charlie, 'pon my word,
    Because, you see, I knew,
From sad experience, many a time,
    What an active wasp could do.

Wall, the statoos snickered, the judges grinned,
    An' Charlie began to shout,
When the Goddess ran for the garden hose,
    An' drowned the varmints out!

But who do you think the judges were —
  All shaved an' drest up fine?
You could n't guess, if you tried a month,
  Who judged this race o' mine :

The Town Hall Eagle, grave an' grim,
  The State House Codfish, tall,
Together with the Hoppergrass
  What roosts on Funnel Hall!

Wall, ev'rything was ready, an'
  The judges hollered " Go!"
An' the way them folks took up the'r legs
  By no means was n't slow!

The Goddess' skirts were so bedewed,
  They checked her for a minite,
An' I began to really think
  The Goddess was n't in it!

But *she* knew what the trouble was,
  An' knew jest what to do!
For she gathered her skirts aroun' her waist —
  An' then she actoolly *flew!*

I can't help laffin' when I think
  Of how she up an' dusted;
Yet 'fore she 'd hardly gone a rod,
  Her corset strings wor busted!

But roun' she went, regardless, at
  A pace w'ich sure must win,
With one han' hold of her headgear, for
  To keep the ha'rpins in!

An' when the others passed the wire,
  Amid the grand hurrah,
They all looked kinder sheepish when
  They found the Goddess thar!

Wall, then she came to whar I sot,
  An' pulled my ears an' nose,
An' thumped my elbows, punched my ribs,
  An' trampled on my toes.

Then I threw my arms around her,
  But she loudly hollered "Stop!"
That woke me up! An' what d'ye think? —
  I was huggin' a *blasted Cop!*

"With one han' hold of her headgear for
To keep the ha'rpins in!"

Page 52.

### XVIII.

Now, out in Wayback County, whar
  I live when I 'm to hum,
We don't have things as you have here, —
  But, Pard, they 're *sure to come!*
Thar 's somethin' *vast* about the West,
  An' somethin' *grand* an' *wild;*
It 's in its infancy as yet —
  But it 's an *awful healthy child!*

*Your* land is mos' too level — now
  My section ain't like this!
You need some grand ole mountains here —
  Ah! them is what I miss!

Ole Natur' builds for us out thar
  Some structur's mighty fine;
An' th' bees 'll hum till kingdom come
  Aroun' each flower an' vine
That grows upon our rugged cliffs,
  In our cañons deep an' brown;
An' th' birds 'll sing till the Master's ring
  Calls the earthly curt'in down!

### XVIV.

What! Goin' now? Why, 'pears to me
  It 's early yet — but no —
It *is* some latish — when folks talk
  How Time does up an' go!

Wall, you 'll find it easy gittin' out —
  Thar was a time 't was *hard;*
You need n't fear no " dead line " here,
  An' you " need n't mind the guard!"

An' Prov'dence willin' (as Parsons say
  When they give the 'p'intments out,
An' tell you whar the Circle meets,
  An' who they 'll talk about) —

Why, I 'll visit you to-morrer, an',
  If in my usual trim,
I 'll eat you out o' house an' hum,
  As sure 's my name is Jim!

But fust I 'll go to a barber-shop,
  An' git my ha'r cut bias,
An' hire a Coon to black my boots —
  An' I 'll look as sweet an' pious

As a Kaffer Missionary — an'
 I 'spect the folks what meet me
Will "strike a gait," an' turn about,
 An' chase me for to eat me!

I 'll fill my pockets with candy 'n' gum,
 An' p'r'aps the small ones may
Be glad to see ole Uncle Jim —
 I 've seen young folks that way!

An' sech a frolic as we will have —
 If the chil'ren ain't *too* small!
I 'll bet my hat your wife will say
 I 'm the noisiest boy of all!

But if anything should happen, Bob,
 We *should n't* meet — why, boy,
Here 's wishin' you lots o' health an' wealth,
 An' lots an' lots o' joy!

Now one more shake! S'cuse my left hand!
 Take care yerself! Good-by! &ast; &ast; &ast;
Wall, who 'd a thought that I 'd see *him!*
 Gee-whiz! How Time does fly!